About the Author
Eun Hee Na has written *Ecology of the Four Seasons, 12 Months of Nature Play, Belly Button Hand, Why Is That?, The World's Scariest Monster, Let's Play in the Forest,* and Foolish Wolf's Book Exploration.

About the Illustrator
Ha Jin Jung studied drawing at Hongik University. She's contributed illustrations for *Spin, Spin, Spin Around, The Cleaner Travels with Mold, and Nursery Rhymes We Share with Children Who Are Learning to Speak.*

Tantan Publishing Knowledge Storybook ***Our Gift-Filled Earth***

www.TantanPublishing.com

Published in the U.S. in 2017 by TANTAN PUBLISHING, INC.
4005 w Olympic Blvd., Los Angeles, CA 90019-3258

©Copyright 2017 by Dong-hwi Kim
English Edition

ISBN: 978-1-939248-21-3

Printed in Korea

Our Gift-Filled Earth

Written by Eun Hee Na   Illustrated by Ha Jin Jung

TanTan Publishing

What fills the vast blue ocean?
Dancing splashes of water!
The ocean is a pool where the fish swim,
and a playground where the birds play.

④ When it is almost dry, the salt is moved to a warehouse on a wheelbarrow.

⑤ Once all of the water evaporates, what is left behind is SALT!

"Wow, it's really salty!"

⑥ Salt is important for making food.
It's needed for preparing cheese, tofu and pickles, making all kinds of sauces, cooking fish and meats, and so much more.

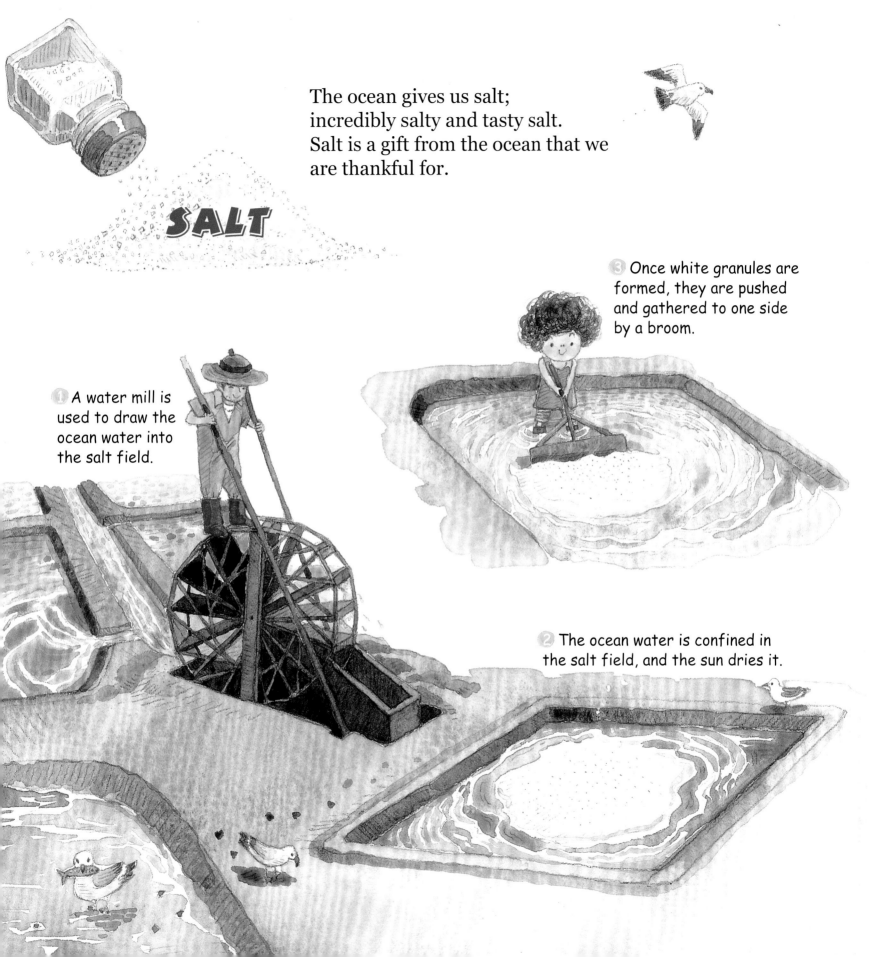

SALT

The ocean gives us salt;
incredibly salty and tasty salt.
Salt is a gift from the ocean that we
are thankful for.

③ Once white granules are formed, they are pushed and gathered to one side by a broom.

① A water mill is used to draw the ocean water into the salt field.

② The ocean water is confined in the salt field, and the sun dries it.

What fills the wide and sparkling beach?
The countless soft and gentle sand!
The beach is a playground for crabs to run around,
and a cozy place where shellfish securely hide.

❸ The liquid sand is taken out and formed into a variety of shapes.

❹ Once it is cooled completely, it becomes GLASS!

❺ When smoothed and flattened, it becomes sheet glass that can be placed in a window frame.
If you blow air into it, it becomes a glass bottle.
If placed in a mold and cooled,
it can become a glass cup or a pretty glass decoration.

Sand gives us glass.
Shiny and perfectly clear glass.
Glass is a gift from sand that we
are thankful for.

1 Sand is mixed with various chemicals.

2 Once this sand mixture is melted in a very hot fire, it becomes liquid sand.

RICE AND RICE CAKES

Rice plants give us rice and rice cakes. Sweet and delicious rice and rice cakes. Rice and rice cakes are a gift from rice plants that we are thankful for.

① After harvesting the rice plants, they are hit on the ground to separate the grains from the stalk.

② The rice grain coverings are hulled in a rice mill, and they become white rice.

③ Wash the rice and boil it in water, and you have RICE you can eat!

④ Rice grains are not just used to make rice. After the rice has been soaked in water,

⑤ It is ground into rice flour.

⑥ The rice flour is placed into a rice steamer and steamed. There it becomes RICE CAKES!

⑦ There are all sorts of rice cakes that we eat: Long and slender rice cakes in the form of a rounded stick, rice cakes steamed on a bed of pine needles filled with powdered red bean, and the rainbow rice cake with an assortment of colors.

What fills the wave-like golden field?
Rows of ripening rice plant clusters!
Rice plants are filling meals for grasshoppers,
and swinging beds on which frogs doze.

What fills the vine-brimming colorful field?
Dangling, swaying, dancing bean pods!
The soybeans are lined up together in the
bean pod.
Soybeans are delicious food eaten by birds,
and bean pods are cradles for caterpillar
larvae to grow.

④ Place brine (salt water) into the soybean water and let it solidify.

⑤ Place the solidified soybean water into a cheesecloth and strain the water.

⑥ Now it is TOFU!

⑦ Tofu is delicious all by itself, but if you pan-fry and eat it or put it in a stew, it's tastier.
If you add water to the soybean water and boil, that's soymilk.

Soybeans give us tofu.
Savory, tasty tofu.
Tofu is a gift from soybeans that
we are thankful for.

③ Boil the strained soybean water twice.

① Soak the soybeans in water, then grind them.

② Place the ground soybeans in cheesecloth and strain.

What fills the rustling white cotton field?
The gently swaying cotton plants!
The cotton field is a vast playground for
bugs, and the cotton is a plush chair for
the bugs.

❹ Place the thread onto a weaving board and weave it this way and that way as it crisscrosses to create cloth.

❻ Choose and draw a design and then cut it out.

❺ Dye the cloth in any desired color.

❼ Following the shape, sew the cloth with a sewing machine. Now they are CLOTHES!

❽ Many different styles of clothes can be created with cotton. Soft underwear, warm thermals, short skirts, long pants, cool tops, and more.

CLOTHES

Cotton gives us clothes.
Snuggly and warm clothes.
Clothes are a gift from cotton that we are thankful for.

❸ Twist the wad of cotton into a long, thin thread.

❶ Pick a cotton plant.

❷ Pull the seed from the cotton plant and wad the cotton.

What fills the sticky wet earth?
Sloppily moving wet soil!
Soil is a blanket that covers animals in warmth,
and gives nourishment for trees and plants to grow.

⑤ Place in a kiln and bake in a very hot fire.

④ Let the clay dry in the shade, then paint it with enamel.

⑥ Now it is POTTERY!

⑦ Pottery is varied. There are large pots, water ladling jars, seasoning jars, steamers to steam rice cakes, and also water pots, oil pots, and more.

Soil gives us pottery.
A cluster of beautiful pottery.
Pottery is a gift from soil that we are thankful for.

① Wet soil is flattened to make clay, and the clay is made round and long.

② Make a round, flat bottom board on top of a potter's wheel. Take the long and rounded clay and wind it around to make each row.

③ Create a shape out of the clay while turning the potter's wheel.

What fills the pasture with spots in every direction?
Dairy cows that take turns saying, "Moo!"
Dairy cows have udders hanging down from their stomachs.
Milk comes out of the udders.
And milk is a calf's delicious meal.

④ Push the solidified milk firmly into a mold to create a shape.

③ Place the congealed milk into a cheesecloth and let the liquid strain out.

⑤ Now it is CHEESE!

⑥ Milk is used to make cheese, but it can be used to make other things as well:
Dried powdered milk, smooth cream, firm butter, sour yogurt, and refreshing ice cream.

Milk gives us cheese.
Cheese that melts smoothly in our mouths.
Cheese is a gift from dairy cows that we are thankful for.

① Squeeze out the milk from the udders of the dairy cow.

② Add vinegar or lemon juice and salt in the hot milk then let it congeal (begin to become solid).

What fills the dense forest?
The wild trees that sway and dance!
Trees are juice bars that bugs frequently
go to, and apartments that animals live
in together.

③ Pour chemicals in with the tiny pieces and boil until the wood becomes melted.

④ Wash and strain the melted wood mixture many times.
Pour in a chemical to make it white.

⑤ After the wood mixture is thinly pressed through a paper machine, it is dried to let the water evaporate.

⑦ Many things can be created with paper. Gift-wrapping paper, calendars, wallpaper, newspapers, and books filled with many different stories.

⑥ Now it is PAPER!

PAPER

Trees give us paper.
Smooth and glossy paper.
Paper is a gift from trees that we are
thankful for.

② Peel the bark of the
tree, and chop it into
tiny pieces.

① Cut the trees from
the forest.

Paper can become a picture book.
A fun book filled with lots of stories.
We read books as we grow up.
Books are the trees' gift that we are
very thankful for!

All these are gifts that Nature has given.
What gifts should we give to Nature?